RESOURCE CENTRE
WESTERN ISLES LIBRARIES

Readers are requested to take great care of the item while in their possession, and to point out any defects that they may notice in them to the Librarian.
This item should be returned on or before the latest date stamped below, but an extension of the period of loan may be granted when desired.

DATE OF RETURN	DATE OF RETURN	DATE OF RETURN
P13 Box 30		
Uiot Bx 7 P1-3		
Jul 15		
		WITHDRAWN

to ----------------------
with lots of love from

----
and
Mimi
xxx

For Ben and Miranda,
with all my love
D.S.

ORCHARD BOOKS
338 Euston Road, London NW1 3BH
Orchard Books Australia
Hachette Children's Books
Level 17-207 Kent Street, Sydney, NSW 2000, Australia
First published in Great Britain in 2005
First paperback publication in 2006
Text and illustrations © Daryl Stevenson 2005
The right of Daryl Stevenson to be identified as the author
and illustrator of this work has been asserted by her
in accordance with the Copyright, Designs and Patents Act, 1988.
A CIP catalogue record for this book is available from the British Library.
ISBN 1 84362 929 1
1 3 5 7 9 10 8 6 4 2
Printed in Singapore
www.orchardbooks.co.uk

Mimi's Magic Wardrobe

The Fairy Party Dress

by Daryl Stevenson

ORCHARD BOOKS

It was Midsummer's Eve, and Mimi had
planned a quiet night at home. She sat
at her garden table with a cup of rosehip
tea and a delicious hunk of cheese.

In the soft light of the
moon, she watched the baby moths
flutter merrily about. What a lovely evening!

But Airy Fairy, Mimi's minuscule fairy godmother, had a very different plan. Mimi was not going to sit in her garden. She was going on a magical adventure.

Airy Fairy began to wave her little wand, sprinkling Mimi with magic fairy dust . . .

Suddenly Mimi was standing
in front of her magic wardrobe!

Carefully, she reached into her pocket and
took out the dainty velvet pouch holding
the wardrobe's golden key.
As she turned the key in the lock,
the doors swung open.

Mimi could hardly believe her eyes.
Shimmering inside was a REAL silk fairy party dress,
with the most delicate fairy wings! Mimi slipped the
dress on. It was simply beautiful! There was a tiny
wand and the most exquisite pair of rosepetal
slippers – a perfect fit.

With a swish of silk, Mimi glided into the wardrobe.

Mimi's heart skipped a beat.
She had a feeling this was going to be
a very special adventure!

The wardrobe began to spin, faster and faster.
When it finally came to a halt and
the doors opened, the sight that greeted
Mimi took her breath away . . .

It was the Fairies' Midsummer Ball!

Every fairy in the land must have been there,
all wearing the loveliest party dresses.
Mimi was so pleased the wardrobe had given
her a particularly beautiful one!

A very jolly band played cheerily and
guests whirled and twirled around the dance floor.

Mimi decided to try out her wings, and
very cautiously began to flutter
just above the ground.

This was FUN! As she got more daring,
Mimi flitted joyfully about, over the band
and around the dance floor.

Then suddenly she heard a familiar voice . . .

"MIMI! MIMI! What are yooo doing?
Ze prince is waiting. Come my little petit pois,
I must introduce yoo to 'im."

It was Madame Frou Frou, dressed in a splendid
stripy ballgown, frantically flying towards her.
She grabbed Mimi's paw and led her down to
where the prince was waiting.

His Royal Highness was dressed in a very
smart coat of the most sumptuous purple velvet.
On his head was perched a golden crown, encrusted
with the deepest red rubies.

Although a little on the small side,
he really was the most handsome fellow.
And, OH, how he could dance!

Mimi enchanted the prince! He guided her over
to his special table where they dined on a
banquet of fairy cakes and sipped elderflower
fizz from crystal goblets. Later, he took her for
a ride in the royal boat on the lake, and
held her hand in the moonlight.
It was soooo romantic!

Then it was time to dance!

They danced and danced and danced,
and the hours flew by, until finally the
clock began to strike midnight. And
sadly, just like in Cinderella's story,
the magic had to come to an end . . .

The next moment, Mimi found herself back in the attic. Her adventure was over. Sleepily, she stepped out of the precious gown. Just as she was about to close the wardrobe doors, she noticed that she had left one of her rosepetal slippers behind . . .

. . . just like Cinderella.